This
MOUSE ■ WORKS
Classics Collection Storybook

belongs to

_____

Disney's 101 DALMATIANS

© 1996 Disney Enterprises, Inc.
Printed in the United States of America
ISBN: 1-57082-045-7
10 9 8 7 6 5 4 3

2

My story begins in London, where I lived with my pet, Roger Radcliff, in a bachelor flat just off Regent's Park. (My name's Pongo. I'm the one with the spots!)

It was a beautiful spring day, and while I sat at the window, my pet made up songs on his piano.

You see, Roger and I were bachelors, which meant that our lives were downright dull. It was plain to see that my pet needed someone, but if it were left to Roger, we'd be bachelors forever.

So when I looked outside and saw the perfect pair heading for the park . . .

I started barking and grabbed my leash. It took Roger awhile, but he finally understood that I wanted to go outside.

Once we reached the park, I searched for the lovely Dalmatian and her pet.

Suddenly I spotted them and slowed down.

Ignoring me, Roger stood near a tree and puffed on his pipe. As usual, it was up to *me* to do something.

I grabbed Roger's hat and dropped it on the bench. Then I turned to look at Roger. When I glanced back, the lovely pair was gone!

I refused to give up.

First, I let Roger snap on my leash, then I yanked
him down the path after the woman. Thinking quickly,
I wrapped my leash around their legs!

My plan worked. Once Roger and the woman untangled themselves, they began laughing. And the beautiful four-legged creature smiled at me!

After a few weeks of absolute happiness, Anita became Roger's bride, and Perdita became mine.

For the first six months or so, we lived in a small house near the park. Nanny, a wonderful cook and housekeeper, came to live with us.

One day, I heard Perdita sigh. "Darling," I asked, "are you all right?"

Perdita smiled. "Of course, dear. After all, dogs were having puppies long before our time."

I don't know who was happier—Nanny or I!

But I do know that all three of us were upset
when Anita's old classmate, Cruella De Vil,
stopped by looking for the puppies.

"It'll be at least three weeks," Anita told
her. Cruella rushed out the door, promising
to return then.

The three weeks passed quickly.
Finally on a stormy night in October, Nanny announced, "The puppies are here! And there are fifteen of them!" she said excitedly.

20

As we smiled at our new family, thunder crackled
outside, and Cruella swooped into the room. "Fifteen
puppies? How marvelous!"

Then she took a closer look. "Why, they don't
have any spots! What horrid little white rats."

As I growled at her, Nanny exclaimed, "They'll
get their spots. You'll see."

"That's right," Anita added. "They'll have their
spots in a few weeks."

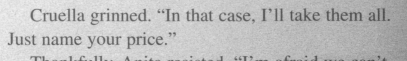

Cruella grinned. "In that case, I'll take them all. Just name your price."

Thankfully, Anita resisted, "I'm afraid we can't give them up."

Cruella ignored Anita and began fiddling with her pen and checkbook. As she splattered ink all over Roger and me, Roger shouted, "We're not selling the puppies! And that's final!"

"I'll get even. Just wait," Cruella hissed as she stormed out.

I found Perdita and the puppies hiding in the broom closet. "Perdy, we're keeping the puppies. Every single one of them."

"Oh, Pongo," Perdita sighed. Then she was able to rest.

As time passed, Perdita and I forgot all about
Cruella De Vil. Instead, we enjoyed watching the
puppies grow.

And when they became old enough, the puppies
especially liked watching the adventures of the brave
dog Thunderbolt on television.

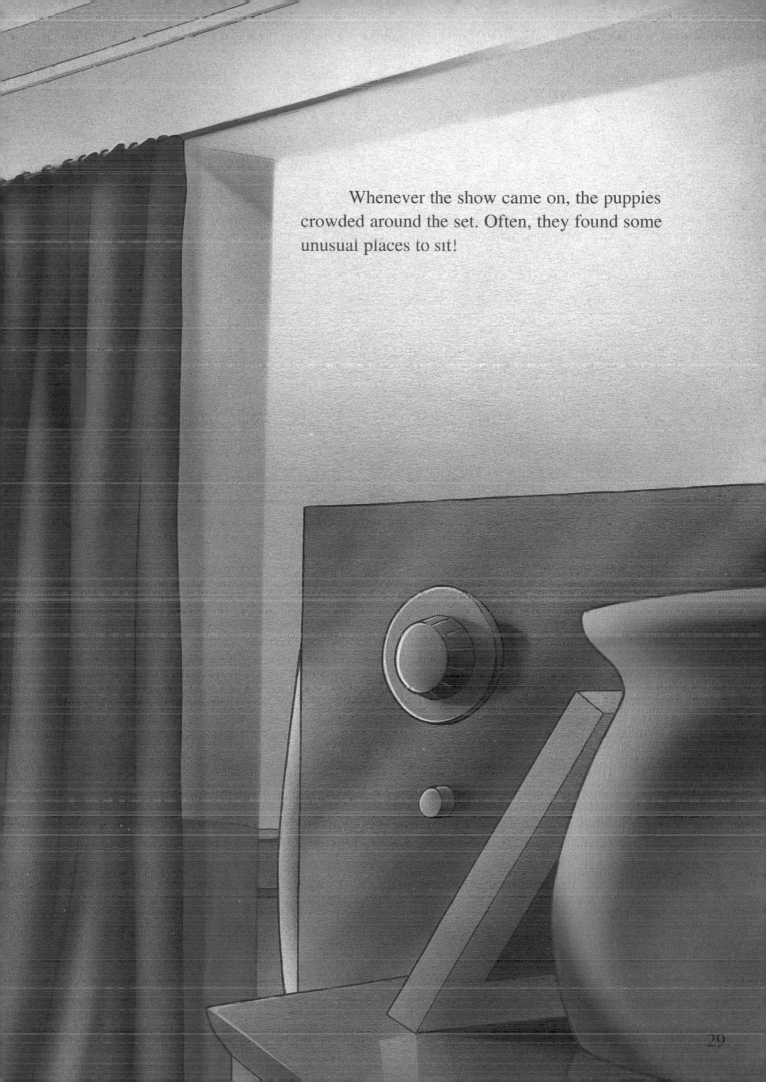

Whenever the show came on, the puppies crowded around the set. Often, they found some unusual places to sit!

Every evening, as soon as the
show was over, Perdita and I kissed the
puppies goodnight. Then, while Nanny
tucked them in, we left for our
walk in the park with Roger and Anita.
Never did we think any harm would
come to our precious little ones.

But one night, as Perdita and I were out with our pets, something terrible happened.

Two evil men, a tall, thin fellow named Jasper and a short, plump chap called Horace, came to the door.

"We're here to inspect the . . . ah, the wiring and switches, Mum," Jasper said to Nanny.

"I don't care what you want to do," Nanny replied. "You're not coming in here!"

But, the two men pushed past her and ran into the house. Nanny tried to stop them, but Jasper locked her in a room upstairs.

When Nanny escaped, she ran to the kitchen.
The basket on the floor was empty. "The puppies!"
she cried. "They took the puppies!"

While Nanny hurried to find the police, Cruella slept peacefully in her house across town.

Later, I learned that when she awoke to the headline in the morning paper, "Fifteen Puppies Stolen–Thieves Flee," she chuckled out loud.

After Roger and Anita had done everything they could, I said to Perdita, "I'm afraid it's up to us. We'll have to use the Twilight Bark. It's the fastest way to send news. If our puppies are anywhere in the city, the London dogs will know."

That evening, as we stood shivering in the park, I barked as loudly as I could, hoping someone would hear me.

Finally, I heard a faint response. "We're in luck! It's the Great Dane at Hampstead."

Then Perdy and I listened as our news was relayed all over London, from the rooftops to the pet shops.

The all-dog alert spread from the city to the country, where a bloodhound named Towser heard it. His friend Lucy asked, "What's going on? What's all the gossip?"

Towser muttered, "Fifteen puppies—stolen!"

Fortunately, Towser sent the word along to the Colonel, an old English sheepdog. A horse named Captain and a cat, Sergeant Tibs, also heard the shocking news.

Sergeant Tibs told the Colonel that two nights ago, he'd heard barking at the old De Vil place.

Sure enough, when the Colonel and Sergeant Tibs investigated, they found our fifteen puppies—along with eighty-four others! Altogether, there were ninety-nine puppies trapped in the house with Horace and Jasper.

At first, we didn't know about the other puppies.
We simply heard that the Great Dane had news, so we
escaped through a bedroom window and hurried out
to meet him.

In the meantime, Cruella drove out to look in on Horace and Jasper. Fortunately, she did not see Sergeant Tibs spying on them from a window.

As the cat listened, he almost fainted. Cruella wanted the puppies for fur coats!

Sergeant Tibs watched Cruella roar away in her car. Then he sneaked into the house and crept up to the puppies. "You'd better get out of here if you want to save your skins," he whispered.

He showed the puppies a hole in the wall, and they began crawling through it, one by one.

54

As the last puppy wriggled through the hole,
Jasper whirled around and shouted, "Horace,
look! They're gone!"

The chase began. Sergeant Tibs led the puppies
down the stairs.

Then he hid them beneath the staircase.
"Here come the men," the cat whispered. "Shhh."
The puppies trembled in silence.

While Horace and Jasper searched for the puppies, Perdita and I looked for the De Vil place. The Great Dane had given us directions, and after a difficult hike through the countryside, we found the Colonel standing outside the run-down mansion.

The Colonel exclaimed, "I'm afraid
there's trouble. Big hullabaloo."

Hearing that, Perdita and I ran to a window.
We could see Horace and Jasper
hovering over the puppies, ready to strike.
Instantly, we crashed through the glass
and attacked.

In a matter of minutes we
overcame the dognappers. As
the men lay dazed and muttering,
we took a moment to cuddle our
puppies. Then, Sergeant Tibs
helped guide us to safety.

We followed the puppies outside, and
Tibs and the Colonel took us to a barn.
It was then that we decided to take the
other puppies home with us.

Soon afterwards, Captain heard a truck coming.
The Colonel graciously offered to stay behind to
deal with Jasper and Horace.
"We'd better run for it," I said.

As we dashed across a field, our brave
friends did all they could to give us a head start.

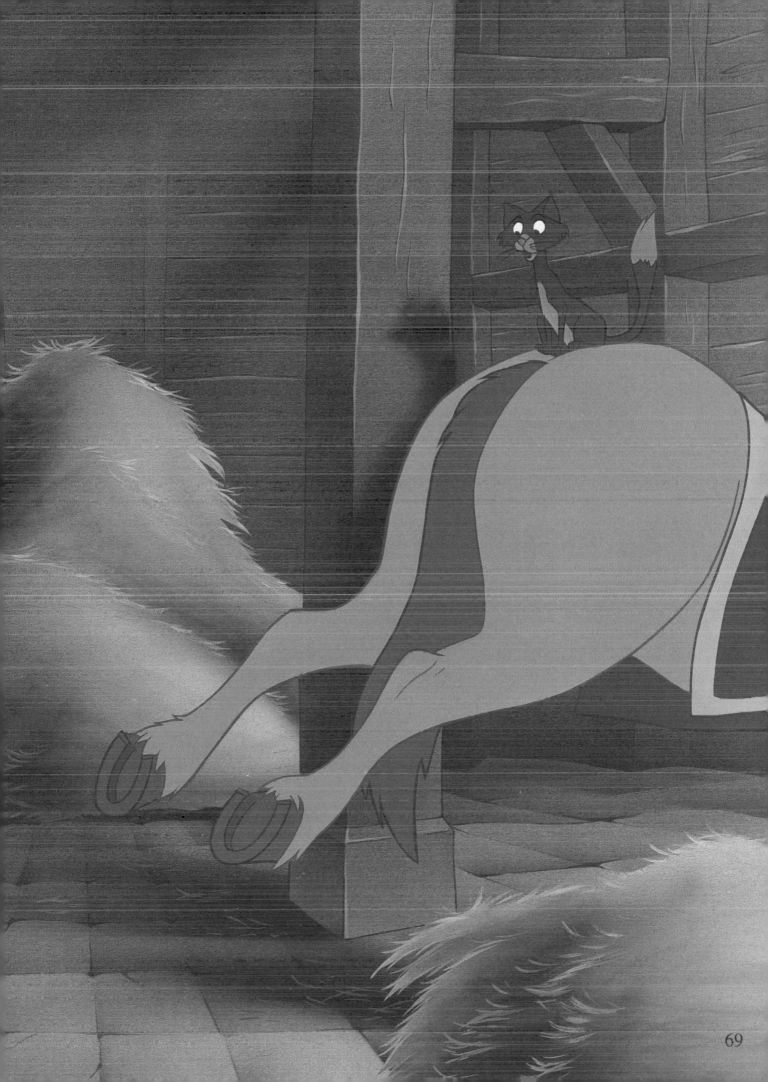

But the men raced back to their truck and followed our tracks in the snow.

I urged Perdy and the puppies to hide under a bridge. We held our breath and didn't move.

Luckily, Cruella's henchmen did not see us.
We waited until they left, then traveled down the icy creek to avoid leaving any tracks.
Just when we thought we couldn't walk another step, we met up with a Collie.

"We'd just about lost hope," the Collie said. "We have shelter for you at the dairy farm across the road."

As Perdy and I led the tired, cold puppies into the barn, four friendly cows gazed at them with concern.

Rolly said, "I'm hungry, Mother. I'm hungry."

"Do they like warm milk?" one of the cows asked Perdita.

"Where, Mother?" Rolly cried. "Where is it?"

Another cow smiled. "Come and get it, kids. It's on the house."

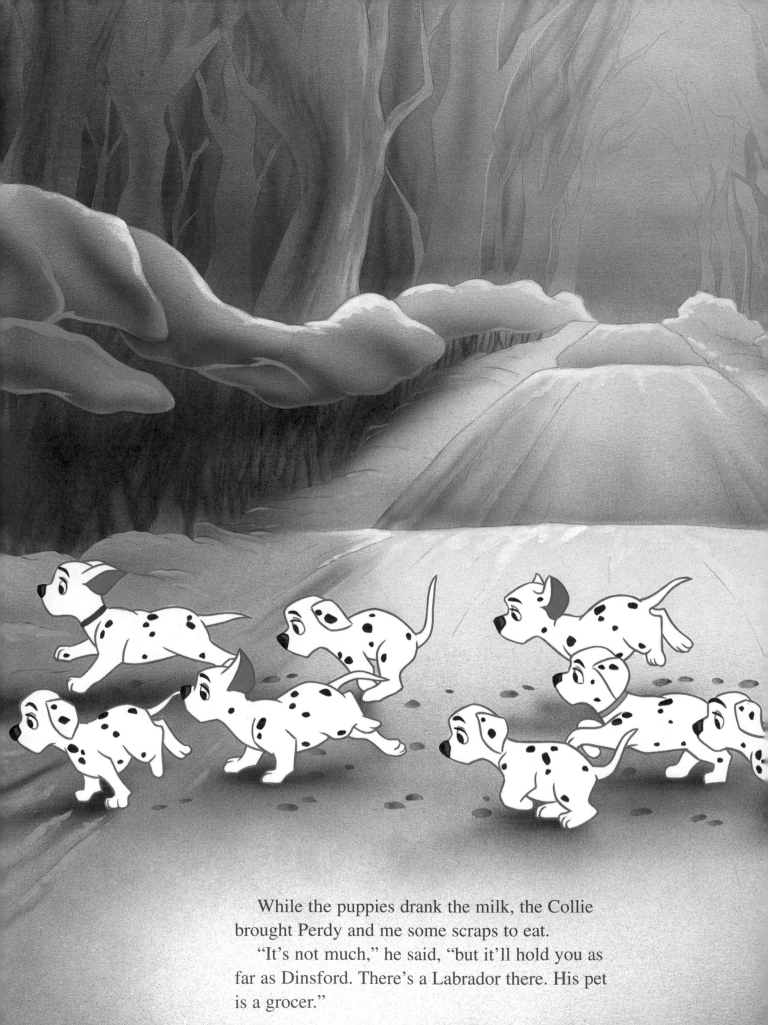

While the puppies drank the milk, the Collie brought Perdy and me some scraps to eat.

"It's not much," he said, "but it'll hold you as far as Dinsford. There's a Labrador there. His pet is a grocer."

As the Collie stood watch, we rested for the night. Then Perdy and I thanked our hosts and herded the puppies outside.

On the way to Dinsford, I heard a car horn honking. "Hurry, kids, hurry!" I urged, guiding them into the woods.

Peering out from behind a tree, I saw Cruella's car screech to a halt. Seconds later, the truck rumbled up with Horace and Jasper.

I heard Cruella shriek, "Their tracks are heading straight for the village. You take the side roads. I'll take the main road."

After they left, we ran through the woods and met up with the black Labrador in Dinsford.

He hid us in an old blacksmith's shop where I got the brilliant idea of disguising our spotted coats with soot.

Soon, we all looked like lovely black Labradors!

Now all we had to do was sneak into the back of a van that was going to London.

While Perdita and I took turns leading the puppies outside, Cruella and her henchmen stopped nearby. I held my breath and hoped that they would not notice us.

Just as we hurried the last bunch of puppies out of
the shop, a large clump of snow fell from the roof
burying one of the puppies.

As I quickly pulled him out, Cruella pointed to the
clean, spotted puppy and yelled, "Horace! Jasper!
They're trying to escape in the van! After them!"

The Labrador helped me get the rest of the puppies into the van. While the valiant dog fought off Horace and Jasper, I leapt into the back and joined the others.

The van took off. Cruella sped after us, with Horace and Jasper taking another route. At one point, she tried to force our van off the road, but the angry driver managed to stay on track.

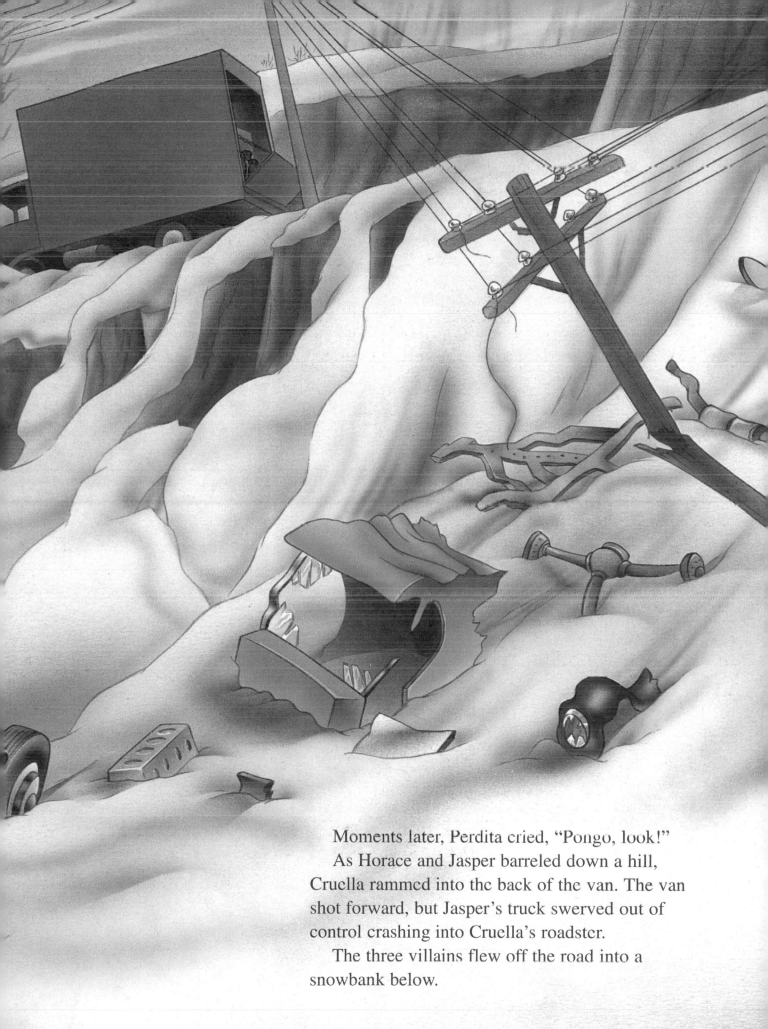

Moments later, Perdita cried, "Pongo, look!"

As Horace and Jasper barreled down a hill, Cruella rammed into the back of the van. The van shot forward, but Jasper's truck swerved out of control crashing into Cruella's roadster.

The three villains flew off the road into a snowbank below.

Safe at last, we settled back into the van. And before we knew it, we were back home in London.

Roger used his handkerchief to wipe off my face, and Anita used her apron on Perdita. "Perdy," she exclaimed. "My darling!"

With a silly grin, Nanny grabbed a feather duster and began dusting off the puppies.

"Here's Patch," she chortled, "and Rolly and Penny and Freckles! They're all here, the little dears."

Then Nanny and our pets began counting.
When they were done, Roger cried, "There's a
hundred and one Dalmatians! Let's keep them
all and buy a big place in the country."
And that's exactly what they did!